# The Adventures of

# The Adventures of

# H.R.H. The Duchess of York
## Illustrated by John Richardson

SIMON & SCHUSTER BOOKS FOR YOUNG READERS
PUBLISHED BY SIMON & SCHUSTER
NEW YORK LONDON TORONTO SYDNEY TOKYO SINGAPORE

SIMON & SCHUSTER BOOKS FOR YOUNG READERS
Simon & Schuster Building, Rockefeller Center
1230 Avenue of the Americas, New York, New York 10020
Text copyright © 1989, 1991 by H.R.H. The Duchess of York
Illustrations copyright © 1989, 1991 by Simon & Schuster Inc.
Box and cover illustration copyright © 1992 by Simon & Schuster Inc.
Music copyright © 1992 by Mike Lobel and Chardiet Unlimited, Inc.
All rights reserved including the right of reproduction
in whole or in part in any form.
SIMON & SCHUSTER BOOKS FOR YOUNG READERS
is a trademark of Simon & Schuster.
Manufactured in the United States of America

10  9  8  7  6  5  4  3  2  1

Each of the four works in this set has been published
previously, individually.

Library of Congress Cataloging-in-Publication Data
York, Sarah Mountbatten-Windsor, Duchess of, 1959-    [Selections. 1992]
The adventures of Budgie / by H.R.H. the Duchess of York :
illustrated by John Richardson.   p.   cm.
Contents: Budgie, the little helicopter—Budgie at Bendicks
Point—Budgie goes to sea—Budgie and the blizzard.
Summary: This compilation of four books about Budgie the
helicopter is accompanied by an audiocassette of the author reading
the stories.
1. Children's stories, English.  [1. Helicopters—Fiction.]
I. Richardson, John, 1955-    ill. II. Title.  PZ7.Y823Ad
1992  ‹Phon Cass›  [E]—dc20  92-11218  CIP
ISBN: 0-671-79249-0

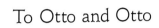

To Otto and Otto

# ~ BUDGIE ~
## The Little Helicopter

It was a hot, hot day. Budgie, the helicopter, was bored. He looked around the huge hangar but nothing stirred. Oliver, the owl, was fast asleep and even Fergus, the cat, didn't notice the mouse in front of his nose. Budgie turned on his radio but nothing was happening.

Every now and then he cooled himself with a whirr of his rotors. "Same old faces," he thought, as he looked around. "I wish something exciting would happen." Budgie always longed for a bit of adventure.

Yesterday Budgie spent the whole day delivering crate
after crate of clawing lobsters from Mulhearn-on-Sea.
"I may be the littlest helicopter," he sighed to himself, "but
I wish I wasn't always given the nastiest little jobs to do."

How Lionel, the Lynx, laughed when Budgie was forced to have a thorough wash and polish afterwards, because he smelled so fishy. There was nothing Budgie disliked more than a good scrub in the helicopter wash.

*Clatter, clatter, clatter, blatter, blatter, clatter.*
Budgie looked up and saw Lionel.
"Hurumph!" Lionel cleared his throat. "Hurumph! Um, this is
Budgie," he said to a small plane who sparkled and shone.

"He's not usually so clean. Must have been forced to wash."
 Budgie blushed red to the roots of his rotors.
"I'm Pippa," said the plane. "I'm new."
"Hello," smiled Budgie.

Bang! Bang! Bang! went the bird scarer. Everyone jumped.
"That's for me. Today is my first flight," said Pippa.
"May I come?" said Budgie. "It looks as though there might be a

thunderstorm and I can warn you if there's any danger of lightning."

"Oh, thank you," said Pippa. "Let's go."

"It's all right for you," groaned Lionel. "Some of us have real work to do."

Pippa soared. She looped the loop. *Wheeee.* Flew on her side. *Brrrr.*

Then swooped. *Eoww.* "Hurrah, hurrah," shouted Budgie. "Well done, Pippa!"

Just then there was a loud noise. *Whoop, whoop, whoop,*
it went. *Whoop, whoop, whoop.*
"That's the alarm," said Budgie.
"Control calling Lionel. Control calling Lionel.

Lionel come in please. Emergency, Lionel. Over."
Budgie clicked on his radio. *Whrrr.* "Budgie to Control,
Budgie to Control. Lionel's out on a job and won't be
back for hours. Can we help? Over!"

"Control to Budgie. You and Pippa are much too light and small. We need Lionel's help. There's a storm brewing."

Budgie looked at Pippa. "Too small?" he said. "Who says we're too small? Too small for what?"

So Budgie listened to his radio to find out what had happened. Rose Wright, on her way home from school in Stanton, was stopped by some men in a car and bundled inside. Now the kidnappers wanted a huge ransom from her parents. Just as he was noting the description of the getaway car, Budgie's radio went dead. The sky grew very dark. The two friends had the same thought at once.

"Come on. Let's go."

Budgie felt the first drops of rain and heard the thunder. As he watched the lightning approach, he couldn't help feeling frightened.

Buffeted and blown, Budgie and Pippa arrived at Stanton. They spotted the school as the rain died away. They didn't know which road the car had taken, so they flew in ever widening circles, keeping fairly low. Then Pippa spied a big, black car in the distance. "Quick," she said. "Let's follow them."

They followed the car for some time. Eventually it turned along a country lane and headed towards an old barn. When the car stopped, Budgie and Pippa flew straight past, pretending that nothing was wrong.

"You keep watch, and I'll go for help," said Pippa. Silently she sped off.

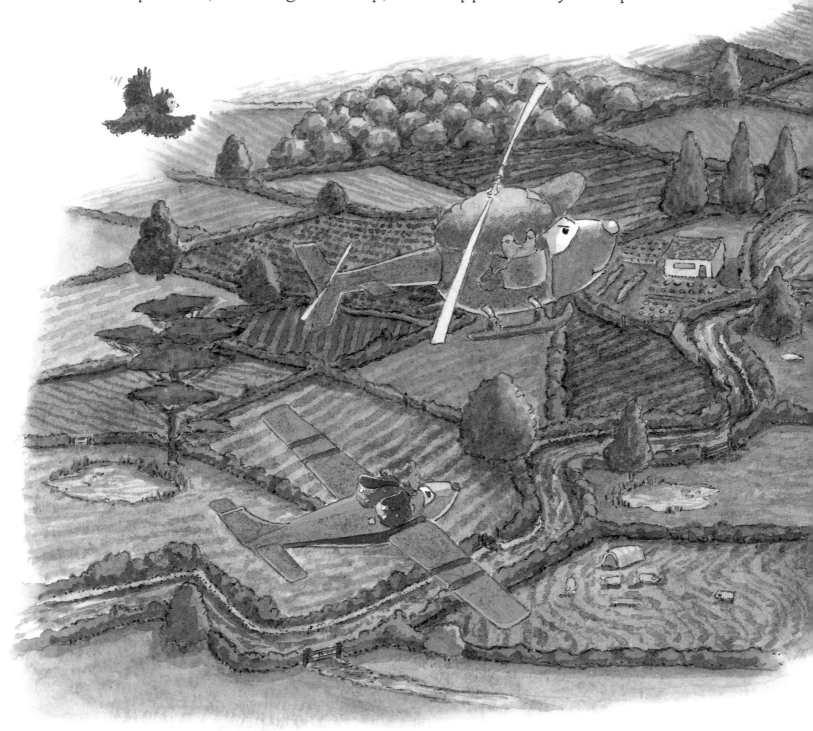

All alone, Budgie flew towards the barn. He turned off his engine and landed noiselessly. "Only a light and small helicopter could land between these trees," he thought proudly. As he watched and waited for help to arrive, it began to get dark.

Bang! Crash! There was a loud noise from the barn. Budgie looked
up and heard a shout. "Get her."

"Over here, Rose!" Budgie shouted. "Look out, behind you. Quick, jump up!"
As quick as a wink, Rose was on board and Budgie went into action.

But just as Budgie lifted off the ground the man grabbed one of his skids and hung on.

"This is my chance," thought Budgie. "I'll keep him dangling until
the police arrive and arrest him. He can't escape."

Minutes later Budgie heard a screech of brakes. The police had arrived and he heard a familiar clatter. It was Lionel barking orders. The second kidnapper made a run for it.

"You won't get far," shouted Budgie.

Then he carefully positioned himself over the roof of the barn.

"Here we go," he said as he shook his skids.

"Aaargh!" Crash! Bang! Splat!

Budgie landed gently and Rose jumped out. Her parents were waiting, happy and relieved that she was safe, and Rose ran towards them. Lionel looked on, smiling.

"Brave little Budgie saved me," cried Rose.
Budgie smiled. "What an exciting day it's been, after all," he sighed
as he started for home.

Back at the hangar, Budgie received a hero's welcome.
"Good work, Budgie," said Lionel.
"I couldn't have done it without Pippa," said Budgie. "We make a good team."

"You'd better come with me," said Pippa mysteriously. "Now you're
a hero, you'll have to be cleaned up."
"Oh no," moaned Budgie. "It's nice being made a fuss of...

...but I hate taking a bath!"

# ~ BUDGIE ~
## At Bendick's Point

*Dring, dring* went the alarm. At last the day of the air show had arrived. Everyone in the hangar was excited. Everyone, that is, except for Budgie, the little helicopter.

"Not much point in **my** getting up," he thought. "I'm going back to sleep."

But Budgie couldn't get back to sleep. Every time he closed his eyes he saw flocks of sheep. Budgie knew it was naughty to chase animals, but when he was out last week he hadn't been able to stop himself. He had hoped no one would see him. Why did Lionel have to fly by just then?

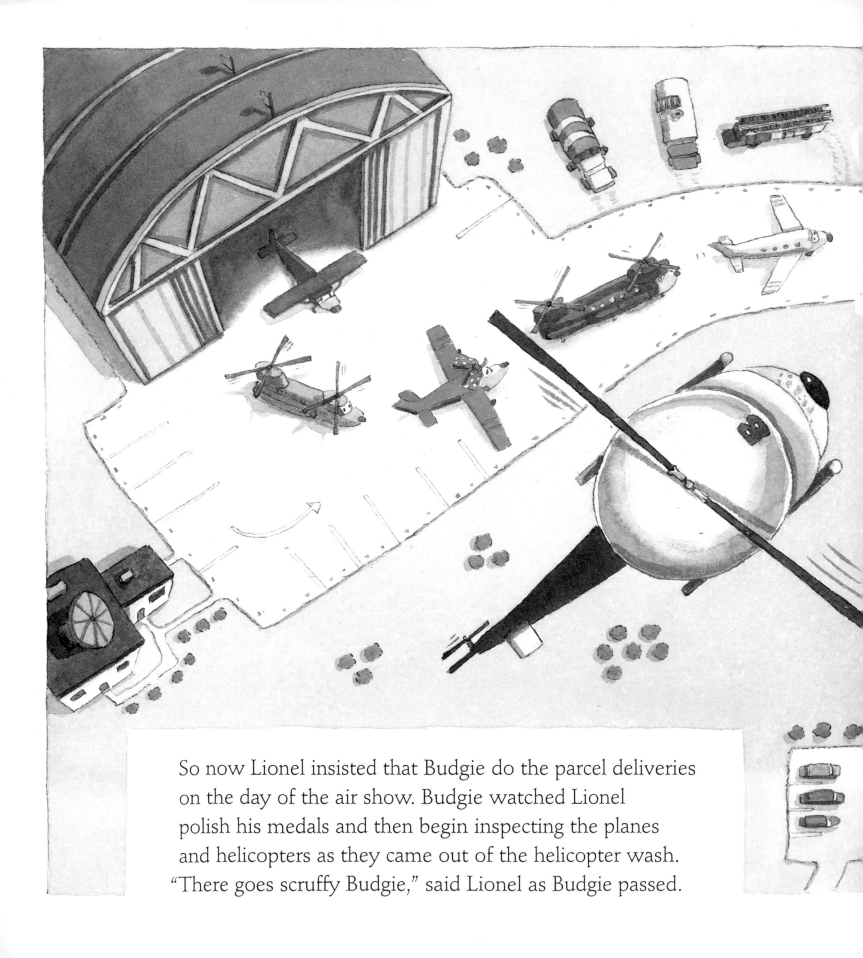

So now Lionel insisted that Budgie do the parcel deliveries
on the day of the air show. Budgie watched Lionel
polish his medals and then begin inspecting the planes
and helicopters as they came out of the helicopter wash.
"There goes scruffy Budgie," said Lionel as Budgie passed.

"I'm glad he's not in the air show, especially my surprise demonstration."

"I don't mind missing the inspection and clean-up one bit," said Budgie, as he rose into the air.

"Bye-bye, Budgie," shouted Pippa after him.

As he flew along the coast towards Bendick's Point, Budgie cheered
up. The sea was sparkling and the cold wind whipped his cheeks.
He almost forgot about the air show and what he was missing.

As he looked down, he saw two boys preparing to go out for the day in their boat. They waved to Budgie as he passed.

As usual, Captain Frobisher was waiting for Budgie when he arrived
at the lighthouse at Bendick's Point.
"Be careful!" shouted the Captain as Budgie lowered the rope. "There's
a gale warning and the wind is getting stronger every minute."
It was difficult to hover, but after two or three tries Budgie managed
to unload his parcels.
"I'd better get on with my deliveries," thought Budgie, "before the
wind gets any worse. They'll be starting the air show about now.
I wonder how it's going."

When Budgie returned, the air show was well underway. But watching the display made him feel left out. "I know," he thought, "I'll listen to my radio. *Helicopter Heroes*, my favorite program, is on." Just then, Budgie's emergency channel came to life. "*Mayday, mayday. Mayday, mayday.*"

"Hold on," said Budgie. "That sounds like Captain Frobisher."

Budgie listened hard. The message **was** from Bendick's Point. The two boys were in trouble. "Quick," said Budgie. "I'd better raise the alarm. I **do** wish Pippa was here."

But as he hopped towards the siren, Budgie realized that no one would hear him. The air show was at its exciting climax with Lionel's surprise demonstration. Lionel and Chin-up, the Chinook, were lifting huge weights on a metal cable. It was breathtaking to watch. Budgie tried to attract their attention but, just then, there was a loud crack.

The cable had snapped! It whipped up and hit Lionel's rotors, knocking him into a spin.

"Oh no," shouted Budgie.

At that moment, Pippa appeared.

The two friends gasped as Lionel made his emergency landing. His rotors were completely bent. The fire engines quickly approached. But Budgie hadn't forgotten

the distress call. He quickly explained to Pippa what had happened. "Come on," he said. "We haven't much time. We'd better go on our own."

Soon Budgie and Pippa saw the familiar rocky coast and Bendick's Point. The gale was getting worse so Pippa circled high above the storm to keep radio contact with the lighthouse. Budgie flew out to sea and then approached the cliffs. He couldn't see much because

the rain beat so heavily into his eyes. At last he caught sight of the
little boat. The boys were trapped in a narrow cove and the tide
was rising. Never had Budgie seen rocks so sharp.
"Good luck, Budgie," radioed Pippa.

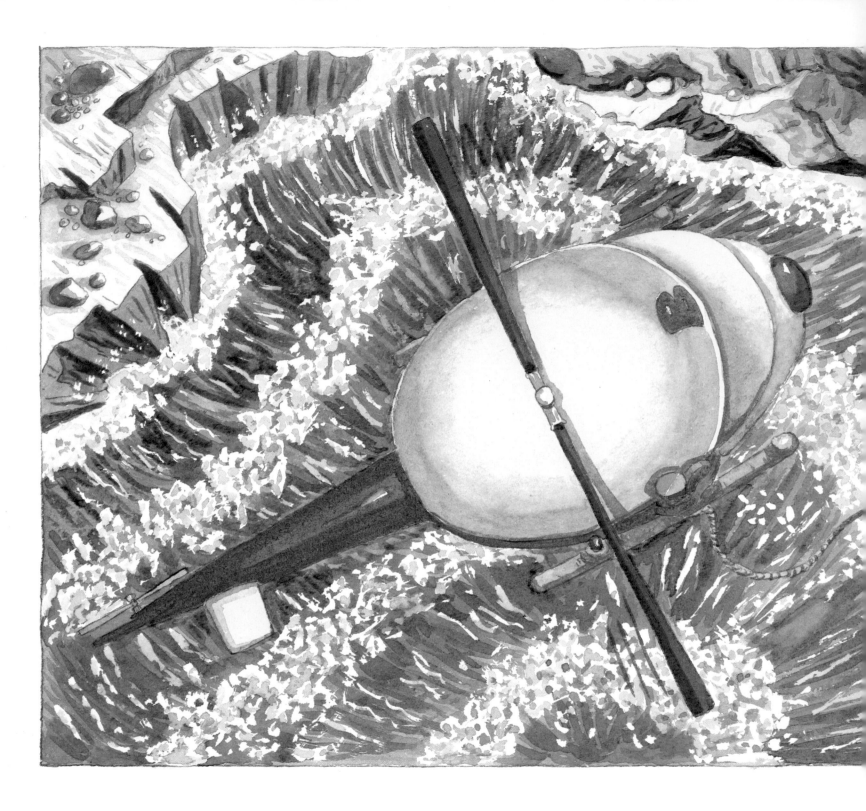

"Help, help!" Budgie heard the boys cry.
"I'd better lower a rope," thought Budgie. "It's our only hope in this
rough sea. Hold on!" he shouted to the boys, but they couldn't hear.

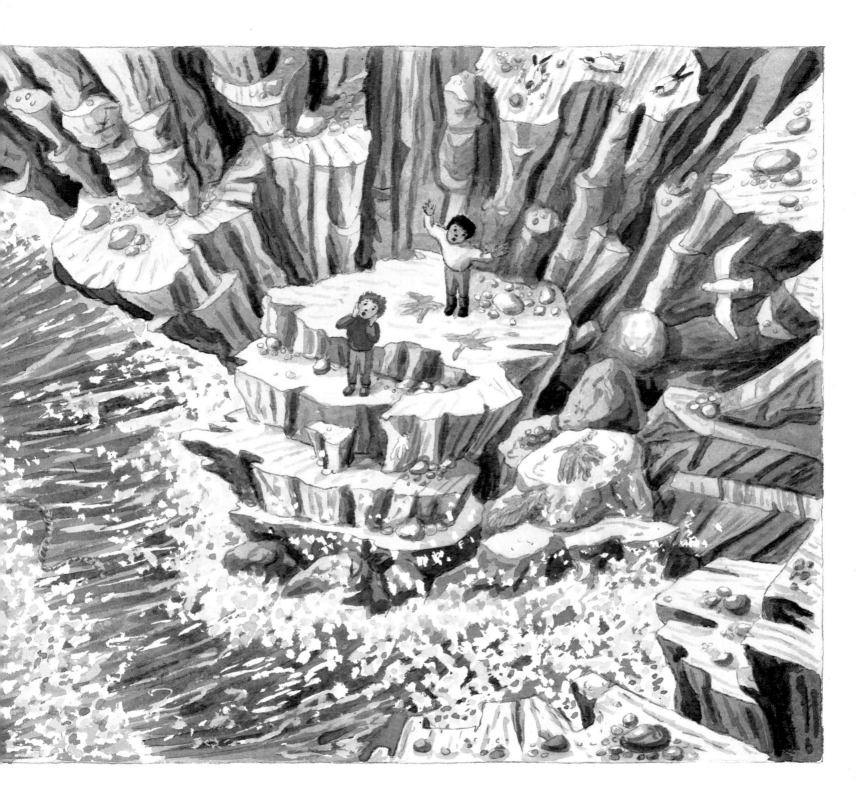

The wind was too strong. All at once a huge, roaring wave hit
Budgie's skids and knocked him off balance. Budgie let go of the
rope and swerved upwards.

The storm was getting worse. "I wish I was back at the hangar," thought Budgie. He looked at Pippa circling above. Budgie knew that a helicopter was stronger in this weather than a small plane. "It's all up to me," he thought. He held his breath as he swooped again into the cove. He hovered for a moment and shouted, "Quick, hang on tight, boys! We're going up."

Using **all** his strength, Budgie rose to the
top of the cliff. Just as he reached safety,
the boys let go of the skids. People rushed
towards them.

"Thanks, Budgie," they shouted.
"It's too dangerous to land here, Pippa," said Budgie.
"Let's go back home before the weather
 gets worse."

On the way back to the hangar, Pippa radioed ahead to tell everyone about Budgie's brave rescue. When the two friends arrived there was a loud cheer. Lionel blushed as he limped forward. "Er… hurumph," he cleared his throat.

"Budgie, you and Pippa have both been very brave." As he spoke, Lionel presented Budgie with a gleaming medal. Budgie beamed.

"And now," said Lionel, "we've got a surprise for you."

Budgie had never felt happier than when he led the flypast.

What an exciting end to an exciting day.

# Budgie

## And the Blizzard

It was early December and a cold wind howled through the countryside. In their snug little farmhouse, Mr. and Mrs. Fairweather were putting the finishing touches on the nursery for the new baby they were expecting to be born in a couple of weeks. Mr. Fairweather finished painting the last wall as Mrs. Fairweather arranged a pretty lace coverlet over the baby's cradle.

"It certainly is cold today," said Mrs. Fairweather. "I just hope
we don't get any early storms," answered Mr. Fairweather. "The
last thing we need is bad weather when we drive to the
hospital."

Mr. and Mrs. Fairweather covered the canary cage, fed the dog, Farckle, and settled down for an evening at home and a long night's sleep.

At the hangar where he lived, Budgie, the little helicopter, was napping in the corner.

"Budgie, where are you?" called his friend Pippa, the Piper Warrior plane.

"Budgie!" shouted the loudspeaker. (It wouldn't have been a loudspeaker if it had whispered.) "Budgie!"

When Pippa finally found him, Budgie was just waking up. "Can't you hear? They've been calling you for five minutes," said Pippa. "Radio back quickly."

Budgie called in and received his instructions. "Just a boring parcel pick up," he grumbled. "Thanks for waking me up, Pippa."

"Next time you have a snooze, don't turn your radio off," scolded Pippa, "and go carefully because it looks like it might snow."

Budgie lifted off at twilight and flew north. Just as it was
getting dark, he saw the railway tracks and followed them. Soon
he saw the station he was looking for in the town at Bradlion.
Budgie landed and asked Mr. Chumpy, the station master, for
his parcel.

Mr. Chumpy frowned. "The train is late and your package is on the train. You can stay here but it looks like a terrible storm is coming." Budgie decided he would wait.

Back at the airfield it started to snow and Pippa
worried about her friend.

Budgie had never been out overnight in freezing
weather, and Pippa knew he hated the cold.

Budgie sat huddled as the weather changed to a full blizzard. He could barely see as the snow drifted over him. The night dragged on. He began to feel very cold.

Early the next morning, even before the sun rose, Mrs. Fairweather woke up with sharp pains in her middle. She nudged her husband. "Michael," she said. "I think the baby is coming a little early."

They both got out of bed, and could hardly believe their eyes when they looked out the window. Everywhere they looked, they could see nothing but white. The fence around their house was buried, their car was buried, and the snow was still falling. They had both slept soundly as the blizzard had raged outside.

"Pack yourself a little bag for the hospital," said Mr. Fairweather, "and I'll go outside and dig the car out."

"Alright," said Mrs. Fairweather, "but do hurry. I don't think it will be very long before the baby arrives."

About fifteen minutes later, Mr. Fairweather came indoors, looking very worried. "I've dug the car out," he explained, "but I can't get the motor to start!"

"Now don't worry. I'll just make a telephone call or two, and I'm sure we'll find a way to get to the hospital on time," Mrs. Fairweather reassured her nervous husband.

Budgie was startled by the call on his radio. "Control to
Budgie. We need your help. We have a woman stranded in her
house who's about to have a baby. You are the only helicopter
available."

Budgie felt frozen, but replied, "Have them put out a signal and give me directions. I'll call in after I take off."

Budgie tried to start his engine. On his third attempt the engine caught but his rotor blades wouldn't move. He was iced up!

Budgie felt terrible. He tried to cheer himself up with a joke: Budgie can't budge. Ha, Ha, Ha. It didn't work.

Pippa had been listening to her radio, and guessed that Budgie was having problems. She could not take off on the snow-covered runway, but thought she could help Budgie anyway.

Budgie was cold and miserable when Mr. Chumpy approached with a steaming bucket. "Some one called and said you might be frozen up," he said as he climbed on top of Budgie and poured hot water on his rotor.

Budgie was so grateful. He thanked Mr. Chumpy for the only bath he had ever enjoyed, and then quickly lifted off.

The snow had stopped and the sun was rising as Budgie flew
toward the Fairweathers' farm.

He searched below and finally saw what he thought must be the signal,
three pairs of bright red long-johns flapping on the clothes line.

Budgie landed in deep snow right beside the farm house. Mrs. Fairweather could barely walk as the couple made their way through the drifts. Finally they were on board and Budgie flew as fast as he could to the hospital. As the Fairweathers went inside they waved and called out, "Thank you! We couldn't have made it without you."

On his way home, Budgie picked up his parcel at the train station. By the time he landed at the hangar, Pippa was so excited she could hardly stand it.

"They had a baby boy," she explained. "They named him Jack
B. Fairweather and the B. stands for Budgie!"
Budgie beamed. "I bet I know who suggested a hot bath for
me. If they ever have a little girl they should name her Pippa."

# Budgie

## Goes to Sea

One day Budgie, the little helicopter, was chatting with his friend Pippa, the Piper Warrior plane. He told her he had been given the exciting new job of postman.

"Nothing exciting about that!" said Pippa. "We all carry mail from time to time."

"But you couldn't do *this* job," crowed Budgie, "because you can't land on a naval ship at sea."

"I could do it easily," said Pippa.

"If you could deliver this mail," protested Budgie, "I'd...I'd have a bath!" Budgie, you see, hated baths. He much preferred being dirty.

"Well," said Pippa, "if the ship is an aircraft carrier, you are going to be very clean indeed."

Budgie worried about that until his radio came on. "Control to Budgie. We have an important shipment of spare parts for the fleet and the wind is beginning to blow. If they don't get these parts, their rescue aircraft won't be able to fly. Please prepare to leave at once."

As Budgie lifted off with his cargo net full, Pippa called to him, "Good luck and I'll see you at the wash when you get back." Fergus, the cat, just sniggered.

"Blatter. Clatter. Blatter." Budgie flew over the coast. The wind
began to blow harder. A line of black clouds hung on the
horizon.

"Control to Budgie. The weather is getting worse. Deliver your parts to the destroyer Camballtown, and return home immediately."

As Budgie approached the destroyer, the wind began to blow even harder. Looking down, Budgie saw that the ship's own helicopter covered half the landing area.

Budgie turned into the wind and began to lower his packages onto the deck. Just as they touched down, a huge gust of wind blew the cargo against the side of the landing platform.

Budgie pulled up with all his might and barely missed crashing into the ship.

"Destroyer to Budgie. That was too close. Land on the aircraft carrier instead."

"Roger," said Budgie, trying to use his strongest voice. He did not want to have a bath, but he did feel a bit shaky from his near miss.

Budgie touched down on the big carrier. The deck was covered with jets. Budgie felt small, but he was proud to be doing his job for the navy.

The crew unfastened his cargo net and Budgie lifted off for
the flight home. As he pulled up, the sky darkened and it began
to rain.

Suddenly Budgie's radio came on. "Man overboard! Man overboard!" Looking down as he flew back over the destroyer, Budgie could see men lowering a lifeboat. He watched as the wind slammed the little boat against the side of the ship.

"Destroyer to Budgie! Destroyer to Budgie! We cannot launch our lifeboat. We have a man overboard and our helicopter is broken. Can you help?"

Budgie gulped. "I'm not big enough for this," he thought, "and the wind is too strong and the waves are huge." But Budgie knew he had to try. He called the destroyer, pretending not to be afraid. "I'll do what I can."

Budgie began to search the sea behind the destroyer. The
waves and the rain made it hard to see anything.

Finally he saw a beam of light. It must be a rescue flashlight,
Budgie thought as he moved closer.

In the sea, the sailor was struggling to stay afloat.

"Keep swimming. I'm going to let down a rope ladder," shouted Budgie as the waves roared below. "Don't give up!"

For a minute Budgie thought he was too late. The sailor had sunk below the surface. Budgie could only see his arm above water.

With the wind howling Budgie dropped as low as he could. He could feel the spray from the waves on his skids. With one final pass he dragged his ladder in front of the sailor.

"Grab hold," Budgie yelled and pushed his engines to full power.

The sailor held on as hard as he could, and Budgie circled back toward the ships.

Budgie lowered the man carefully to the ship's deck as all his mates cheered. Once his ladder was released, Budgie immediately lifted off and flew toward home. The wind was still very strong and Budgie just hoped he could make it back to the field.

When Budgie finally arrived there, Pippa, Lionel the Lynx helicopter, and Chin-up, the Chinook, were waiting. They had heard everything on the radio.

"We are all *so* proud of you," cried Pippa.

"Hurumph," Lionel said, "that wasn't a bad job Budgie."

"Grrreat stuff," said Chin-up as he chewed his gum.

After everyone had finished praising Budgie, he had a chat
with Pippa.

"Pippa, you won our bet. You could have landed on that aircraft carrier. I guess I'd better have that wash now."

"I could never have saved that man, Budgie," Pippa said, "so I'm calling our bet off."

Now this was a special day indeed thought Budgie. All this adventure and no bath before bed!